DATE DUE

Miami
Sees It Through

Then I hear Miss Spraggins saying, "What about you, Michael Andrew? Do you understand?"

"No, ma'am," I say. Now, I'm meaning, *No, please don't call me Michael Andrew,* but she's thinking I'm saying, *No, I don't understand.*

Miss Spraggins is not with me on this. "I see," she says. "So you're a smarty-mouth. Then see if you can understand this. Michael Andrew, you have detention."

"What? But—"

"Not another word, young sir."

Who's ever heard of getting detention on the first day of school? I've got a sinking feeling—fourth grade is busted!

To James Everett.
Welcome.
—P.M. & F.M.

To Ms. Davis, 6th grade,
Lemont Elementary.
—M.C.

Miami
Sees It Through

by Patricia & Fredrick McKissack
illustrated by Michael Chesworth

A STEPPING STONE BOOK™

Random House 🏫 New York

www.randomhouse.com/kids

Library of Congress Cataloging-in-Publication Data
McKissack, Pat.
Miami sees it through / by Patricia & Fredrick McKissack ; illustrated by
Michael Chesworth. — 1st Stepping Stones ed.
   p.   cm.   "A Stepping Stone book."
SUMMARY: Miami Jackson and his strict new fourth grade teacher, Miss
Spraggins, get off to such a bad start that Miami is determined to transfer out
of her class, even if it means leaving his friends behind.
ISBN 0-307-26513-7 (pbk.) — ISBN 0-307-46513-6 (lib. bdg.)
[1. Teachers—Fiction. 2. Schools—Fiction. 3. African Americans—Fiction.]
I. McKissack, Fredrick. II. Chesworth, Michael, ill. III. Title.
PZ7.M2173Mi 2004 [Fic]—dc21 2003025075

Printed in the United States of America   12 11 10 9 8 7 6 5 4 3 2

Contents

1
First-Day Blahs

Tuesday, September 8, 7:35 A.M.

It's the first day of school, not my favorite day of the year. And I've got the first-day blahs. Summer's over. No more late-night movies. Time for homework. But on the other hand, I can't wait to see all my friends.

My best friend, String, is in his usual spot—at the kitchen table. I'm busy packing my backpack, putting in fresh pencils, new notebooks, clean paper. Everything is neat. String's pack is already a mess inside. Two things about String nobody can forget. One, he loves to eat. But as much as he eats, he's still as skinny as a shoestring. That's how he got his nickname—String. And two, he's a mess. His desk, his backpack, his room at home. They are all a mess!

String and I have been knowing each other like forever. We watch old movies, ride bikes, play ball, and go to camp and stuff together. We share most everything. Since he's an only child, I even let him borrow my sister, Leesie, when he needs somebody to hassle.

"Hey, guys," Mama says, yawning as she comes into the kitchen. She pours herself a cup of coffee and thumbs through a music journal. Mama's teaching afternoon classes this semester at the junior college. Mornings will be much calmer, because Mama's not rushing to get out of the house at the same time we are. "So how do you two feel going into fourth grade?" Mama asks. "Got a new teacher, too."

Miss Amerita Spraggins was supposed to teach fifth grade, but our teacher moved away. Now Miss Spraggins has taken over the 4T class. I met her in the store this summer and she acted like a marine drill instructor.

"What is our new teacher going to be like?" I say, thinking out loud.

Just then, Daddy and Leesie come into the kitchen from the garage. It's good to have Daddy in town. His construction company is building a parking garage for a local hospital expansion project. So he won't be away this fall as much as he was last spring.

"I've checked the car and everything

should be fine," Daddy says, wiping his hands on a towel.

Leesie thanks Daddy and gives him a gushy kiss on the cheek. She can be so syrupy at times.

My sister is a senior at Kirkland High, a cheerleader, and all of that other popular girl stuff. If Leesie were in the dictionary, her definition would read:

LEESIE: a strange mixture of emotional drama; has the personality of a soft summer rain that can morph into a hurricane a minute later.

Leesie's been a cool breeze lately. The reason? A car.

Leesie worked all summer at a local ice cream store. Daddy matched her dollar for dollar and she bought a new car. Well, it's not a new car. It's an old one, but it's new to Leesie. So what's the catch? Mama okays the deal, if Leesie agrees to drive String and me to and from school every day. Leesie agreed quick and in a hurry. We know the truth, though.

My sister would rather drive two dead flies to school than us. That's why we're going to rub it in even more, by riding in the back and making it look like we're being chauffeured.

"Time to go," Leesie tells us. "Can't be late the first day." Her fake smile is working overtime.

"Be careful," Daddy says, his face filled with concern. "You have your license? Got the insurance card? Got your cell phone? Call me if anything goes wrong. Anything. Promise?"

"Promise." Leesie hugs Daddy and

throws Mama a kiss. "I'll be responsible. Really. I'll show you."

String and I crack up. Leesie? Responsible? Please.

8:00 A.M.

Leesie rolls up in front of Turner Elementary and brakes. She dumps us out, shouting, "Be right here after school or else!" She pulls away, turning the corner and running over the curb. That's my sister . . . the storm.

Everything at Turner looks the same, feels like before. Fresh paint job, but the color's the same. Mr. Hillshire, the principal, is standing out front greeting students the way he has as long as I can remember. He's surrounded by a herd of jumping, screaming kindergartners.

"Hey, man," says Horace, one of my partners. He catches up with us at the door. We speak to Mrs. O'Shay and a few other teachers.

"What's up?" says Willie, another friend. We all high-five and continue down the hallway together.

"Well, if it isn't the four monkeys—hear, see, know, and *do* nothing right." Who else could it be but Destinee Tate?

I've known Destinee Tate all my life, too. And as much as I like String, I hate Destinee Tate. She goes out of her way to make life miserable for me. And her sock-puppet friends, Amika and Lisa, are just as bad.

Somehow String gets along with all the girls—especially Destinee. He talks to them and treats them all nice. Still, he's my best friend. What's wrong with this picture?

"Somebody told me you'd transferred to another school," I say to Destinee.

"What school?" she asks.

Got her! "The Lassie Come Home Obedience School." Horace and I high-five.

"I'm really too tickled to laugh," Destinee sneers. Then in the same breath, she speaks to our new teacher in a drippy sweet voice. "Hello, Miss Spraggins." I'm sure there is a course they teach girls at night when we boys are asleep: How to turn on the charm when you need to con a grown-up.

"Good morning," Miss Spraggins says stiffly. Destinee doesn't know what to think. No gushy smile. I'm thinking this lady might be ah-right if she can read Destinee's game.

Then I speak. "Hello, Mrs. Spraggins."

"*Mrs.* Spraggins was my mother," she answers. "She's no longer with us. But I'm *Miss* Spraggins. Good morning. Welcome. Please go in and have a seat, immediately."

Welcome? *Welcome!* I don't think so.

2
Detention!

Same day, 1:00 P.M.

The first-day blahs have turned into the first-day bust. The cause? Miss Amerita Spraggins, our teacher. She's worse than a 1950s B-movie monster. She's worse than a bad toothache. Worse than a rainy Halloween. Worse than my main enemy, Destinee Tate.

Everybody who knows me knows I hate nosy, fussy, pushy, disgusting Destinee Tate. So what does Miss Spraggins do? First, she puts Destinee in the seat right behind me. Then she assigns Rashetta Lewis the desk in front of me.

Last year, String finally got me—and the other guys—to stop picking on Rashetta about her runny nose. So she's got allergies. I can hang with the sniffing, as long as she puts her tissues in the trash can. But no way am I sitting in front of Destinee Tate all year. That's asking a brother to do too much.

Truth is, I'm missing Ms. Rollins, our teacher last year. She let us sit where we wanted for the first week or two of school. You know, to get a feel for the room. *Then* she made a seating chart and *then* the desks we selected became permanent. But not Miss Spraggins. No! We come in the first day—our seats are assigned. No argument.

Destinee and I both complain about the seating arrangement.

"I can't sit in front of . . . of . . . *her*," I say, frowning.

"And I'm not sitting behind Peanut-Head, either," Destinee snaps back.

Miss Spraggins gasps, like she's having a fit or something. Then she lets us have it. "I will not tolerate name-calling. You will sit in your assigned seats and be civil to one another. Do you understand, Destinee?"

"I understand," Destinee answers, softly.

Then I hear Miss Spraggins saying, "What about you, Michael Andrew? Do you understand?"

"No, ma'am," I say. Now, I'm meaning, *No, please don't call me Michael Andrew,* but she's thinking I'm saying, *No, I don't understand.*

Miss Spraggins is not with me on this. "I

see," she says. "So you're a smarty-mouth. Then see if you can understand this. Michael Andrew, you have detention."

"What? But—"

"Not another word, young sir."

Who's ever heard of getting detention on the first day of school? I've got a sinking feeling—fourth grade is busted!

3
Not Like Ms. Rollins

Wednesday, September 9, 9:45 A.M.
Slow day. The first few days of school usually are—filling out forms, getting books assigned, meeting with the counselor, and whatever. But this morning Miss Spraggins laid down the law.

If we're late without an excuse, she'll give us detention. If we run in the hallway, talk when we should be working, or get up to sharpen a pencil without permission—detention. The list is posted on the bulletin board so we have to look at it all day.

Now, Ms. Rollins used to give us three demerits before we got detention. Not this lady. First offense and Miss Spraggins strikes like a bolt of lightning.

Ms. Rollins was the best teacher ever.

But I've decided no more detentions for me. I got lucky yesterday. Didn't have to tell Mama and Daddy I got detention. Leesie had to check out her cheerleading uniform for Friday's football game. So she was late picking us up. Responsible, huh? String and I acted like we had been waiting for a long time.

11:45 A.M.

Our 4T lunchtime is from 11:45 to 12:15. Then our recess is from 12:15 to 12:45. As usual, all the girls sit together and all the boys sit together at lunch. Amika and Lisa, the sock puppets, are up to their regular routine—following behind

Destinee. But even they aren't doing much giggling today. They got detention for talking.

None of us boys feels like doing much eating either—except String. He'll eat in the middle of a tornado if the table is set.

At recess, it's too hot and humid. Who feels like playing ball? Nobody. The fourth-grade girls aren't even jumping rope or playing hopscotch.

"Maybe they're missing Ms. Rollins," Horace says, shaking his head. When school ended, she left to teach at a school in Ghana, West Africa. They're lucky kids. We're stuck here with Miss Amerita Spraggins.

"Everybody loved Ms. Rollins," I add.

"Miss Spraggins isn't as pretty as Ms. Rollins. Not as nice, either," says Horace.

"And Miss Spraggins is old, old—way over thirty," I say.

"Yeah," We-the-People puts in. "She even drives an old car."

We're on a roll with *old*.

"Miss Spraggins talks old, and even says she's a teacher from 'the old school,'" David, another one of the boys in 4T, chimes in.

"I wish she'd go back to *old* Boston and teach *old* English, at that *old* school. Then my life could get back to normal," I say. We're all laughing now. Feels good.

Meanwhile, I'm noticing that String isn't saying much. "What's up with you?" I ask.

"Ummm," he says, munching on a carrot stick left over from lunch. "Maybe we shouldn't be so hard on Miss Spraggins. I

mean, she's new here. And maybe she's scared."

We're all silent. Then we crack up laughing. "Get serious, String! Miss Spraggins scared? Of what?"

String shrugs, the way he does when he's clear about something and he's trying to help you get it, too. "She's from Boston," he says, popping a mint into his mouth.

"And . . . ," I put in.

"And she hasn't taught school in over ten years. She was taking care of her sick mother. Then her mom died. That's scary. I would be scared if my mom died and I was living in a new city."

"How you know all that stuff about her?" Horace asks.

"Miss Spraggins told me some. While I

was waiting for you in detention, Miami, we got to talking. And I also overheard my mom—she's the PTA president—talking about it. That's all."

Whatever. I'm not buying it. "Who ever heard of a teacher being scared?"

4
The Name Game

Same day, 2:45 P.M.

The second day is almost over! We are covering our new books with plastic. The covers will look like new, but the insides will still be raggedy.

I don't feel like covering my books. I can do it at home later. So I put my head down on the desk.

Miss Spraggins the Dragon strikes. "Michael Andrew, sit up straight. That's a desk, not a bed."

Why does she insist upon calling me Michael Andrew? Nobody, I mean nobody in the world calls me Michael

Andrew—not my parents, my friends, or even my grandfathers, whose names are Michael and Andrew. Only Miss Amerita Spraggins does.

My nickname has been Miami since String couldn't say my nickname, which was Mike Andy. It came out Mi-a-mi. I guess my nickname has a nickname. And I like it. It's a really special thing about me. There are three Michaels in my class, but I am the only Miami I know. But I can't make Miss Spraggins understand that.

She insists, "Your given name is what's on your birth certificate. Robert, not Bobby or Robbie or Rob. Elizabeth, not Liz, Beth, or Liza."

That may be true. But everybody knows that Christopher Tyler is String's "real" name, and who calls him that? Michael

Keller has been We-the-People since the day he confused the Pledge of Allegiance with the Preamble to the Constitution.

The other kids don't seem to care. But I do. I'm still trying to make her understand. "*Miss* Spraggins," I begin, trying to be polite. "Miss Spraggins, you want your name to be said correctly. Why won't you use the names we want? I'd like to be called Miami."

"Don't you know when to shut up?" Destinee Tate whispers. Everybody hears her. Some kids start giggling.

"Leave it alone," whispers String. I'm not listening to any of them.

Miss Spraggins sighs. "I see you're upset. Please let me explain. Your name is who you are. Your parents gave that name to you. It is the most important possession you have. Whenever you do business in this world—when you apply to college, buy a car, or open a bank account—you will be expected to use your legal name, not a nickname."

Has Miss Spraggins ever heard of Hank Aaron, Babe Ruth, Tiger Woods, and President Teddy Roosevelt? Anyway, she's talking to the whole class, not just me now. I'm the only one talking back.

"But Miss Spraggins," I say, "we're just in fourth grade. We've got a long time before we apply to college or buy a car."

Miss Spraggins has a look on her face that's saying she's getting ready to slam-dunk a detention on me. You can't be a teacher unless you master THE LOOK—the one that can stop a charging rhino dead in its tracks.

"Do you have a library card?" she asks slowly.

I nod.

"Speak your answers," she insists. The Dragon never lets up.

"Yes," I say out loud.

"What's the name on the card?" She's giving me THE LOOK.

"Michael Andrew Jackson."

"That's my point exactly." She folds her arms and looks satisfied.

I am going too far. I know it, but I can't stop myself. "Yeah," I say, "but the librarian calls me Miami."

"Michael Andrew . . . detention!"

5
How Bad Is It?

How bad is it? I've got detention for the third day in a row. Destinee Tate. She poked me in the back and I yelled "ouch" 'cause it hurt. Miss Spraggins gave us both detention. Lisa and Amika got detention for talking again. You'd think they'd learn to keep their mouths shut.

Miss Spraggins has us water all the plants. Then I feed Tibbles the turtle. He reminds us that a turtle gets the job done by being patient and persistent. Tibbles has been our class mascot since first grade and gets promoted with us each year.

Meanwhile, String is watching out for Leesie.

Miss Spraggins decides that she wants to talk. She asks Lisa about her hobby.

"I got a camera for Christmas last year," Lisa says. "I like to take pictures."

Miss Spraggins nods her approval. "You'll have to bring some of your pictures to class. Perhaps we can make a display."

Lisa goes all smiles. "That sounds great, Miss Spraggins."

Amika says she likes sewing. Miss Spraggins suggests that she might lead a project to make a new night cloth to put over Tibbles's tank.

"I'd like that," says Amika.

Then she asks Destinee what she likes. "Baseball. I love baseball," she says.

Hey! That's my answer.

"I went to baseball camp in June and played on the all-star team." Destinee goes on and on about the championship team. She never mentions String, Horace, We-the-People, or me. We were there, too. The only reason why she even heard about Camp Atwater was because of String.

"Do you think the Yankees will go all the way this year?" Miss Spraggins asks. I can't believe she even knows people play baseball.

"Their bats are hot," says Destinee, trying to sound like she's in the know. "And with the strong pitching they've got, they're sure to win again."

Miss Spraggins turns to me. "Now, Michael Andrew, what interests you?"

It's baseball! But I can't say it, because

it'll seem like I'm copying off of Destinee. "I don't know. Nothing, I guess."

"Nothing?" Miss Spraggins seems surprised. What I mean is, *Nothing interests me more than baseball*. But probably Miss Spraggins is thinking I mean *Nothing interests me*. Too late to explain.

"All of you are dismissed," she says. I'm out of there. I can almost see the smoke coming out of her nose. Miss Spraggins and I are like bad Jell-O. The kind that when you mix it up, never gets firm. We aine solid.

3:26 P.M.

String has kept Leesie from coming inside to get me, making up one excuse after another. Leesie is upset. "You're almost fifteen minutes late. Why?"

I try to play it off.

Leesie isn't buying it. "Come on, little brother. 'Fess up. Or would you rather I tell Mama—no, Mama *and* Daddy—that something's not right here?"

"Okay. Okay, Miss Law and Order. My teacher gave me a detention. I got one yesterday and today."

Leesie is shocked. "What for?"

"Miss Spraggins doesn't like me," I tell her. "That's how come. She is nothing like Ms. Rollins. Everything I say or do is wrong."

"Is she that bad, String?" Leesie asks.

String thinks for a minute. Then he snaps his fingers and it's like a light switching on in his head. "Okay. Okay. Okay," he says rapidly. "Remember the first few weeks in third grade? We thought Ms.

Rollins was too skinny and too stuck-up to be a good teacher."

"Yeah, but we found out we were wrong. Really wrong about her," I say.

"Miss Spraggins might be ah-right like that, too. We just maybe need to get to know her better."

"You say that about Destinee Tate all the time," I come right back. "But the more I get to know her, the worse she gets. Miss Spraggins will be like that, too. I know it."

"Whatever," says Leesie, pulling off. "Miami, if Mama finds out about your detentions, you're going to be grounded forever."

How bad is it? Try a dozen rotten eggs mixed with garlic. It stinks!

6
A Solution

Same day, 4:00 P.M.

String and I are fixing a snack before I help him move his mama's ferns inside. Leesie's going to the library to study. "I've been thinking . . . ," she says.

"Uh-oh," says String.

"This is square business. Listen up. Why don't you ask Mama and Daddy to let you transfer to another class?"

"What?" I'm so used to Leesie's dumb ideas that when she comes up with a good one, it takes a minute to process.

"Hey, that could be the solution. I *could* go over to Mr. Harvey's 4C room. Then I'd be rid of Miss Spraggins. What do you think, String?"

String pops the last of a cookie in his mouth. "I don't know," he mumbles as he munches.

5:30 P.M.

Leesie gave me something to think about. Moving out of Miss Spraggins's room feels right to me.

"We've got to figure out a way to get our parents to let us change over to Mr. Harvey's room," I tell String, all excited.

"Us?" he answers. "I'm not moving anywhere. That's your idea."

At first, I'm thinking he's not for real. Then I see that he is. "Why not? You're my best friend, and best friends stick together."

"You are my best friend. And best friends do stick by each other. That's why you shouldn't go running off to another class."

"I'm not running. I'm escaping. That's different."

String shakes his head.

"What?"

7:00 P.M.

Dinner's over. Dishes done. Floor swept. Trash taken out. Mama's in the family room looking over music for the junior college course she's teaching on twentieth-century composers.

String or not, I'm going for it. I go in and flop on the couch. "Mama?"

"Yes," she answers, not looking up.

Silence. Maybe this is not the best time.

"Oh, nothing." What should I say?

Silence.

Mama looks up. "Are you okay?" She's eyeing me for signs of what might be wrong. "Are you feeling sick?" Mama touches my head. It's cool. I'm not cool inside, though.

"Is something wrong at school?" she asks, looking right in my eyes. I look away. Why do I do that? It's a sure sign she's guessed right.

Taking a deep breath, I just let it all out. "It's Miss Spraggins," I say. "Our new teacher. She's awful."

Mama is surprised. "Tell me about it."

"Miss Spraggins is bear mean, fire-breathing-dragon mean. All the time snapping orders, never giving an inch, handing out detentions like coupons."

"That mean, huh?"

"Yes, and more," I add. "I've been thinking . . ." I sit up and look right in Mama's face. "I would like to move to Mr. Harvey's fourth-grade class."

Mama's eyebrows come together in a serious expression. "My goodness, you *are* unhappy."

Right away, she calls Daddy. I repeat the story to him—about the nickname stuff, the detentions, all of it. Then they send me to do a chore. That's when they talk. About fifteen minutes later, they call me into the family room.

"Open House is a week from Monday," says Mama. "We want you to stay with Miss Spraggins for one more week."

"One more week?" Well, at least they didn't say no.

Mama goes on. "After the week is over, if you still want to transfer to another class, then we'll talk to Miss Spraggins and Mr. Hillshire."

I know the answer to that right now. Once I'm in Mr. Harvey's class, I'll be rid of Miss Spraggins . . . and Destinee Tate, too.

7
Sold?

I can't wait to tell everybody I'm changing
to Mr. Harvey's 4C class. But when I do,
they all act like I'm going to Egypt.

"Why you moving, man?" Horace asks.

"To get away from Miss Spraggins,
that's why," I answer. "You can move, too,
if you want."

"Mr. Harvey might not be any better
than Miss Spraggins," We-the-People
says. "No, thanks. I'll take my chances
where I am."

Horace says the same thing. "I'll hang
in 4T."

11:48 A.M.

By lunchtime the whole class knows I'm moving to Mr. Harvey's.

"Deserter," Lisa hisses at me as we go through the lunch line. "Our class has been together since kindergarten."

"Yeah, traitor," chimes in Amika. "And you're getting ready to mess up everything by moving."

Rashetta's even hanging out with them now. "Some of us . . . a few people . . . your friends will miss you if you leave."

After I tried to be nice to Rashetta. This is my thanks.

I try to blow them off, but Destinee blocks my way. "Not so fast, Mr. Quitter," she says.

That does it! "I'm not a quitter. Moving is good strategy. The way a ballplayer

44

moves when he and the coach don't click."

"You really don't get it, do you?" says Destinee.

Lisa puts her hands on her hips. She moves in close. "String is your ace buddy. And you haven't noticed how upset he's been?" She stomps her foot.

"Yeah," says Destinee. "We all are—I mean, everybody has been upset. Besides, who'll be the class idiot if you leave us?"

The girls laugh as they walk away. I'd move to Antarctica to get away from Destinee Tate.

5:20 P.M.

Made it through the week with no more detentions. Looking forward to the weekend. No more Miss Spraggins.

I'm feeding Shimmy and Shammy, our

pet fish, when Daddy comes in. "The house on the corner is sold," he says, tossing his keys on the kitchen counter. "They're painting and fixing it up." He pours himself a glass of juice, then pours one for me.

Leesie comes down the steps. Curlers are bobbing around on her head like pink sausages. White sticky goop is smudged over her face in patches. She's getting ready for Kirkland High's first football game of the season. Getting ready is always a production for Leesie. Every strand of hair has to be in place before she'll put her toe out the door.

She hears just enough to comment. "You mean the old spookity house on the corner is sold? Wonder who bought it?" she asks.

"Wonder *why* somebody bought it," I say.

Daddy laughs. "It really is a lovely Victorian farmhouse. Roomy, well built. Wait and see what it looks like after they finish the paint job. I think your opinion will change."

Leesie is not convinced. Me either. Mama comes into the kitchen from the laundry room, carrying a stack of folded clothes. Leesie plucks her white turtle-neck from the pile. "Did you say the house on the corner is sold?" Mama asks.

"I hope a family with lots of boys who love baseball move in," I say.

"Me too. Lots of big, handsome boys," says Leesie, grinning. The white goop on her face has dried and is cracking.

"Help!" I yell, pointing at Leesie like I

see something awful. "Help her. Her face is falling off!"

She chases me to my room.

11:59 P.M.

I'm in a deep sleep when a knock comes at my door.

"Who goes there?" I call out, the way military guards do when they're on duty.

"Me?" It's Leesie. She's whispering.

"Advance, 'Me,' and be recognized," I respond as usual.

She rushes in, still dressed in her cheerleading uniform. She switches on the light next to my bed. "What? What's up?" I ask, rubbing my eyes.

Leesie is walking back and forth, rumbling like thunder. The storm is coming. She's mad, and her hands are shaking.

She's scared and mad—a bad combination.

"How am I supposed to see a dark blue car rolling in the pitch-black dark without any lights on?" she's saying.

"Hey, wait," I say. "Start from the beginning. What car? Where? Did you have a wreck?"

Leesie takes a deep breath. "You're not going to believe this. Okay. Here's what happened. I took Marquisha home after the game. Then I'm on my way here. When I turn the corner to come into the subdivision—*wham!* Out of nowhere, there's this car pulling out of the driveway of the old house on the corner."

"The empty one?"

"It isn't empty anymore! To keep from hitting the car, I have to turn into the hedges. By the time I stop, I'm halfway into the yard." She's breathing hard and still really scared.

"Hey, chill, Leesie. Calm down."

She takes a couple of deep breaths, then settles down enough to tell me the rest.

"Hold on. There's more. I get out of the car. There's no damage. I'm not hurt or bleeding or anything. But out of the darkness comes this lady. Her arms are flailing like a flag in the wind. 'Look at my hedges,' she says. 'You drove right through them.'"

Leesie flops on my bed. "By now, I'm upset, okay? So, I say to her, 'Ma'am, I'm sorry. You were backing out just as I turned the corner. I ran into your hedges to keep from hitting you.'"

Leesie sits back up, reliving the moment in her head.

"She asks me my name? I tell her, 'Leesie Jackson. I live down the street.' 'No, what is your real name?' she asks."

Uh-oh. That sounds too familiar to me. There is a twitch in my stomach as Leesie goes on.

"I tell her, and then I ask her name. 'Amerita Spraggins,' she says. 'I just bought this house. I'm moving in this weekend.' Oh, Miami, she's as awful as you say she is!"

I fall back on my pillow. Spraggins the Dragon is going to be my neighbor.

I can't wait to tell String about Leesie's run-in with Miss Spraggins and that the Dragon Lady is actually moving into our hood. Talk about bad luck!

8
Abbreviated Lesson

Monday, September 14, 8:18 A.M.

For once we are all in our seats on time and before the bell rings. We've got a new intercom this year, so we can hear without a lot of crackling and popping. A sixth grader is reading over the lunch menu and making other announcements about the first scout meeting and a reminder that next Monday is Open House. All I'm thinking about is getting through the week.

Miss Spraggins taps a ruler on her desk to get our attention. "Class," she says, scoping the room with dragon-radar eyes.

"You studied abbreviations last year. As a quick review, we are going to solve a mystery."

Ordinarily, I would love a mystery, but with Miss Spraggins, who knows?

"Someone has snatched Tibbles the Turtle." We all look. His tank is missing. "They left us this note." Miss Spraggins writes the clues on the chalkboard:

You'll find Tibbles the Turtle
In the hands of a well-known Ste.
Across the st. of St. Louis
On St. St. near the So. 1st St. Sta.

"It's eight-forty-five. You have one hour to rescue Tibbles. Remember your class motto: Patience and Persistence. The clock is ticking!"

"May we work in teams?" Destinee asks.

Miss Spraggins agrees. Of course Destinee forms a group with Amika and Lisa. String, Horace, We-the-People, and I make a group.

9:00 A.M.

We read the clues again. "I don't get it," says Horace. "All those streets and saints don't make sense."

"Let's take it line by line," suggests We-the-People.

You'll find Tibbles the Turtle
In the hands of a well-known Ste.

String gets the abbreviation dictionary. He looks up *Ste*.

"*Ste* is the abbreviation for a French female saint," he says. "So the mascot can be found in the hands of a well-known lady saint."

"Way to go," I say. We move to the next clue.

Across the st. of St. Louis

"That's easy," says Horace. "*St.* is the abbreviation for street and saint. So that line should read: across the street of Saint Louis."

"In the hands of a well-known saint across St. Louis Street," says We-the-People. "That's downtown."

We move to the next line.

On St. St. near the So. Ist St. Sta.

We study the clues. I look over at the girls. Their heads are together. Destinee looks confused. Good. Meanwhile, Miss Spraggins is walking around the room listening to our conversations. She's standing behind our group.

On a hunch, String looks up *st*. "Look

here," he says. "*St.* is an abbreviation for stanza and stone, too."

Miss Spraggins smiles and nods.

We're on to something. "*St. St.* could be Stone Street or Stanza Street," I say. We look at a city map. We find Stone Street. Now we look up *Sta.*

"*Sta.* is the abbreviation for station. And *So.* is short for south," String tells us. "The South First Street Station was a railroad station, but now it's a restaurant."

So that clue means: *The statue we're looking for is on Stone Street near the old South First Street Train Station, which is now a restaurant.*

We use a telephone directory, a city map, and a history of St. Louis to help us with the clues. "Stone Street runs north and south," I say. "Moving south, Stone

58

Street crosses South First Street, then St. Louis Street."

String traces the lines on the map. "On Stone Street, between South First and *near* St. Louis Street, there's a church named Ste. Genevieve," he says.

"Out front is a statue of Ste. Genevieve. That's a lady saint," Horace says, finding a picture of the saint. "Her hands are outstretched."

"We've found Tibbles!" we shout.

"We have, too," says Destinee.

"We said it first," I say.

"Quitter," she whispers.

9
An Unexpected Visitor

Same day, 4:00 P.M.

String and I are watching a dorky horror movie when the doorbell rings. Everybody who knows us uses the side entry that leads to the kitchen. This must be a stranger. The doorbell rings again. Suddenly, Leesie rips into my room.

"It's her," she says. Leesie's got scared-chicken movements. She's fluttering every which way. "Miss Spraggins. Oh, Miss Spraggins. I'll never get to drive again."

"Oh, man." A million thoughts are running through my head. Is she here to get Leesie or to do me in?

Mama opens the door and Miss Spraggins introduces herself as a new neighbor. Leesie, String, and I creep to the upstairs landing, where we can see and hear what's going on in the living room and not be seen.

Mama introduces herself and says, "You teach my son, Miami—I mean Michael Andrew."

I close my eyes, not knowing what to expect.

"Yes, I do. Michael Andrew is . . ." Miss Spraggins pauses, then adds, ". . . a spirited boy. To be honest, Mrs. Jackson, we haven't gotten off to a good start."

I can feel my stomach doing a gymnastics routine.

"Partly, it may be my fault," she continues. "I know education has changed since

I last taught ten years ago, but some things never change. Lessons that teach good manners, discipline, respect for self and others, being tidy, being on time—these lessons are as important as math and literature."

"Oh, I agree one hundred percent," Mama says.

"Perhaps I have been pushing too hard in that direction. Michael Andrew will do fine. He's a bright young man and very well liked by his peers." Then, taking a deep breath, Miss Spraggins adds, "But that's not why I stopped by."

Leesie is squeezing my hand so tightly, it's about to break. "I've really come about your daughter, Alyssa."

Leesie groans softly.

"The other evening, I forgot to turn on

my car lights. I was backing out of the drive. At the same time Alyssa was turning the corner. Alyssa showed good judgment to avoid an accident. She quickly swerved her car into some nearby hedges. I was quite shaken and went on about the hedges, completely forgetting to thank Alyssa."

Leesie eases up on my hand some. Her mouth is hanging open. If she knew how funny she looks, she'd close it with a quickness.

Mama thanks Miss Spraggins. "Leesie—Alyssa—didn't say a word to us about the *almost* accident. I'll call her down. You can speak with her yourself."

We dash back to my room. "Did you hear that?" Leesie is so relieved. "Did you hear her say I used good judgment?"

Leesie is fluffing her hair like she's going onstage. Mama calls. "Coming," Leesie sings. Before going down the steps, she throws a whisper back to me. "I thought you said Miss Spraggins was psycho? She sounds okay to me."

What does Leesie know? Anybody who uses her name and "good judgment" in the same sentence is not from this solar system.

"See? Miss Spraggins didn't skank on you," String puts in. "In fact, she said nice things about you."

"Why are you all the time on her side?" I ask.

He shrugs. "I'm not siding with anybody. I just think you should give Miss Spraggins a chance. "

Silence.

"Help, help, help! Get away from me!" the woman in the video shouts. I click her off mid-scream.

I think I've finally got it. String is saying he wants me to give Miss Spraggins a chance because he doesn't want me to move to another class.

I'm not worried. If I move, String will come on over with me.

10
The Dragon's Backyard

I have to admit, yesterday was surprising. First, I liked the mystery abbreviation review. Miss Spraggins has a way of teaching math that's really cool, too. Next, Miss Spraggins didn't come down hard on me to Mama. And she really does know baseball, even umpired one of our games at recess. But just when I'm thinking String might be right about her, she blows it.

"Miss Spraggins?" I say, remembering the abbreviation review.

"Yes, Michael Andrew."

"An abbreviation is a short version of a

68

word. Like *st.* is short for street. Right?"

"Yes, sir." Miss Spraggins is so prim and proper.

I go on. "Sort of like Mike is short for Michael?"

"Yes, Michael Andrew," she says.

Miss Spraggins's face is sliding into THE LOOK. She knows where I'm going with this. The whole class knows where I'm going with this.

"Then you might say abbreviations are like nicknames for words. Right?"

Miss Spraggins is giving me the complete LOOK. Then, slowly, her face changes like one of those *Star Trek* shape-shifters. Now she's looking . . . thoughtful?

At last she speaks. "Interesting! Michael Andrew, I never really considered abbreviations from that point of view. But you're right. Abbreviations are shorter spellings of a word—much like a nickname."

Should I go on? Yes? No? *Yes!* "So, if it's okay to use abbreviations, then why not nicknames?"

String shakes his head. Horace covers his face. We-the-People closes his eyes. All the girls give me a dirty look.

But Miss Spraggins never skips a beat. "Of course abbreviations can be used . . . in informal writing and some poetry. You never use them in a formal letter or a report. The same applies to nicknames. The classroom is a formal setting. Your friends and family may call you by your nickname at home, but at school I will always use your proper given name. Does that answer your question?"

Destinee leans over. "Zap! Wap! A big

fat slap in your face," she whispers. "Miss Spraggins is right on. Give it up, Michael Andrew," she says.

I hate Destinee Tate.

4:00 P.M.

"At least Miss Spraggins didn't give you detention. You know how she is about nicknames. Why'd you bring it up again?" String says later.

"There you go, taking sides again."

String does a Rams' Marshall Faulk move—a quick sidestep and straight up the middle. "Look, I'm helping Miss Spraggins plant tulip bulbs. Mom volunteered me," he says.

"Gag time. How could your mother do that to you?" I ask.

"Miss Spraggins called your mother,

too. But she was at work. So my mom went and volunteered you."

Whacked!

"Look, I'm not helping *her*, I'm helping *you*," I say as we walk up the street to the Dragon's backyard.

Once there, I check things out. See how Miss Spraggins lives. No bones lying around. In fact, the house has been freshly painted. Like Daddy said, it does look a hundred times better than before. And the yard is looking good, too—very prim and proper, like Miss Spraggins.

We knock on the door just as Destinee Tate comes around the side of the house.

"What? Where'd you come from? Why are you here?" I ask.

"My mom brought Miss Spraggins a welcome basket from the PTA today. And then she volunteered me to stay and help plant bulbs."

"We don't need your help," I put in.

"Hey, I'm not excited to be here."

Suddenly, Miss Spraggins swings open the door. She greets us with a face full of smiles and a bag full of tulip bulbs. She also has a drawing of her yard. There's a spot for all different kinds of flowers. She tells us about her idea.

"I appreciate your help with this project," she says, handing me a few bulbs. "I only expected Christopher and Michael Andrew. I'm so glad to have you, too, Destinee."

While we work, Miss Spraggins asks us about ourselves. Before we know it, we're telling her about summer baseball camp. I finally get to say that baseball is my very favorite sport in the entire world.

Then Miss Spraggins describes her garden in Boston. "There was always something blooming, from early spring until the first frost," she says. You can hear her missing it.

"Do you miss Boston?" Destinee asks.

Duh! Of course she does.

"I lived in Boston all my life. I lived in the same house all my life. I have friends there. Some I've known since kindergarten. I miss them very much."

"I bet they miss you a whole lot," String says.

Miss Spraggins doesn't answer quickly. At last, she says, "My friends miss me, but they are still together, able to see each other, share good and bad times *together*. And I am here, alone. I'm not lonely, for I have my work and my new house and garden. But I must admit I get a little homesick sometimes." Then she perks up. "This area is going to be sunshine on the ground come March."

We finish putting in the final bulbs just before the rain starts . . . a slow hot-chocolate-afternoon rain. We hurry into Miss Spraggins's kitchen. We're sitting at her table while she nukes four cups of cocoa. She serves them with marshmallows floating on top while we listen to the Red Birds play their final game of the season.

Okay. So she's not a complete dragon.

11
The Decision

Wednesday, September 16, 12:20 P.M.

I've been thinking about what Miss Spraggins said about her friends.

At recess, while we're waiting for our turn at bat, I ask String, "You'll really miss me when I move to Mr. Harvey's class, right?"

"Yep," he answers.

"Then why don't you move to 4C with me?"

"You're my best friend, Miami," he answers. "But you aren't my *only* friend. I like my class. And I would miss my other friends if I were away from them. Just like

Miss Spraggins. I'd be lonely without you. But I'd be even lonelier without We-the-People, Horace, Destinee, Willie, Amika, and all the others. Besides, you'll only be just across the hall."

I knew that.

The next morning, 7:27 A.M.

Woke up this morning with my mind made up.

I'm staying in 4T with kids I've known all my life. I've had it all wrong. Sure, my friends would miss me. But I'm the one who would be miserable, wondering what they were doing and working on. They are my friends—almost all of them. Besides, who would hate Destinee Tate if I left?

"How's school going?" Mama asks for the umpteenth time. She sits down to have cereal with me. If she's not asking, then it's Daddy. "Doing okay in school, son?"

"School is school," I say, putting my books in my backpack. "Oh, I've made up my mind to stay in 4T. Final answer," I say, being as cool as I can.

Mama tries to turn away, but I catch her mouthing, YES!

"Good choice," Daddy says, slapping me on the back. He's all grins, too. "I'm proud that you've decided to see it through."

"So, li'l bro, you gonna hang with Miss Spraggins," Leesie puts in. "Told you she was okay."

"You're the one who told me to move out of her class!"

"I admit, I was wrong."

Leesie doesn't mean that. She's just putting a con on Mama and Daddy that she's *ma-tur-ing*. That's her word for the week.

8:25 A.M.

My friends are glad I'm staying around. "You finally got it," says Horace.

"At last," says Willie.

"Glad that little piece of drama is over," Destinee says.

Even Lisa and Amika seem okay that I'm staying. "You've got some sense after all," says Amika.

Surprise!

Rashetta hands me a note. It says, "I'm so (spelled with a dozen o's) glad you're not leaving." Then she turns around and smiles at me. She's got a dimple. Funny,

I've never noticed it before.

I don't know what to say. So I just look dumb.

4:15 P.M.

String and I stop by to see if Miss Spraggins needs any help in her yard. We figure we can use the extra bucks with the holidays coming.

We're helping her unpack boxes while listening to the ballgame. "The Dodgers are up 3 to 1 in the bottom of the fifth," she says.

Miss Spraggins is amazing. We swap baseball talk about the Red Sox, the Cardinals, coaches, stats, and what's going on off the field. But actually, basketball is her favorite sport.

"I played basketball in college," she

says, showing us a picture of her in uniform. "Guard."

She's also got tons and tons of books. "I love to read," she tells us. I believe her. It's going to take at least seven bookcases to hold her books.

We work until it's time to go home for dinner. String runs ahead. I stay a bit longer. Just got to say something that's been on my mind since yesterday.

"Say, Miss Spraggins." I'm not sure how to put it, so I blurt it out fast. "Can we start over? I didn't like you at first, but you're okay now."

Man, that didn't come out right at all. I'm wondering what she's thinking when she stands up. She puts her hands on her hips. Here it comes. "I appreciate your honesty," says Miss Spraggins. "And yes, we can start over." Then she laughs.

She's got soap-detergent eyes. They get lighter and brighter as her smile gets bigger. And when she's smiling, "Michael Andrew" won't sound wrong or strange or out of place. It will sound . . . like Miss Spraggins. I've decided that I'll try to keep her smiling.

"See you tomorrow," I say.

Miss Spraggins smiles again and says, "Good-bye . . . Miami."

About the Authors

Pat and Fred McKissack find inspiration for many of their characters in their own lives. Miss Amerita Spraggins is based on several teachers Pat had while growing up, and on one in particular. "She was prim and proper at all times," Pat says. "We thought she was an old fogey, but we found out she was much more than that. She was a wonderful teacher."

Fred adds, "I've had teachers like Miss Spraggins in my life, too. They would teach math and then play kickball at recess."

In 2001, Pat received the Virginia Hamilton Award. She is the author of many books for kids, including the Caldecott Honor Book *Mirandy and Brother Wind* and the Newbery Honor Book *The Dark-Thirty*. Together, she and Fred wrote *Christmas in the Big House, Christmas in the Quarters*, which won a Coretta Scott King Award.

MIAMI Gets It Straight

There goes Ms. Rollins, standing beside the door to Room 16. She's been greeting our third grade, Class T, the same way, every day, all year. And there go all the girls hanging around her. Sucking up. Especially the chief suck-up, Destinee Tate.

She's like the leader of the girls. A real bride of Dracula. I guess I'm sort of like the leader of the boys. The girls think the boys are all maggot brains. We're too cool for them, that's all!

Just five more days of Destinee Tate and the rest of the girls in 3T. Then I don't have to see them all summer.

MIAMI Makes the Play

Kenneth flops his bag on the top bunk. This guy looks tough enough to hit a ball to the far side of tomorrow.

"That's my bed," says Taylor. "There's a bottom bunk left over there."

"You take it," says Kenneth, scowling. "I want this one." Taylor backs down.

But String speaks right up. "Hey, wait. Keep your bed, Taylor."

Kenneth turns toward String. His red hair seems redder. His green eyes seem greener. "Oh yeah! Who says?"

"Hey, man, chill," says String matter-of-factly. "Take my top bunk. I'll take the one over there. It's only a bed."

Looking at Kenneth, all I can say is, "Mission Control, we've got a problem."